DEC. 2013

To KATIE

OM HEATHER & KIZZY

MERRY XMAS

XX
OO

FAIRY
PRINCESSES

FAIRY PRINCESSES

TALES OF THEIR MAGICAL SECRET WORLD

Written by
NICOLA BAXTER

Illustrated by
BEVERLIE MANSON

ARMADILLO

This edition printed in 2006

ISBN-10: 1-84322-300-7
ISBN-13: 978-1-84322-300-9

3 5 7 9 10 8 6 4

Published by Armadillo Books, an imprint of Bookmart Limited, Registered Number 2372865 Trading as Bookmart Limited, Blaby Road, Wigston, Leicester LE18 4SE, England

Produced for Bookmart Limited by Nicola Baxter
Designer: Amanda Hawkes
Production designer: Amy Barton
Editor: Sally Delaney

Printed in Singapore

Contents

Princess Rose's Secret

Princess Rose was a real princess, but she didn't feel like one. It was true that she lived in a palace. It was also true that her father was a king and her mother was a queen. She had three princess sisters, too. But Rose looked at her sisters and felt somehow different. They loved being princesses. They liked dancing and pretty clothes. Rose wasn't so sure. She felt happiest outside, in the shady woods and gardens around the palace.

One day Princess Rose discovered that she really *was* different, and in a most wonderful way...

It was a sunny spring morning. As usual, Princess Rose had escaped from the palace before the royal golden breakfast plates had been cleared away. She ran out into the gardens, where flowers were shyly raising their heads towards the sun, and dew drops glittered on the grass.

Princess Rose sighed with happiness. Just then, she heard a call from the palace.

"Princess Rose! Princess Rose! Time for your deportment classes! Madame Noon is here! Your sisters are waiting!"

The voice was faint. Rose could hardly hear it. The idea of spending such a beautiful day indoors, parading up and down the stairs with books on her head, filled Rose with horror. She hated deportment lessons. They were supposed to make her walk and sit and dance like a princess. But deep inside, Rose didn't want to be a princess. She just wanted to be herself.

Rose turned sadly. She didn't want to go, but she simply couldn't pretend she hadn't heard. She stood for just one more moment and closed her eyes, trying to remember the sounds and scents of the gardens.

It was then that she heard, for the very first time, a wonderful sound. It was a bird, singing nearby. The pure, high notes rolled towards her like perfect pearls. Rose felt the song swirling around her. It made her forget Madame Noon and her sisters. It made her forget she was a princess. The song was so beautiful that she could think of nothing else. As she opened her eyes, Rose saw at once a little golden bird, sitting on a branch. As he sang, it seemed as if the whole garden turned to listen.

Slowly and softly, Princess Rose walked towards the golden bird. He didn't seem afraid. In fact, it was as if his song was drawing her onwards. "Follow me, follow me," he sang. "Follow, follow, follow!" As if in a dream, Princess Rose moved silently forward. She realized that she was passing between two trees, whose trunks and twining branches made a kind of archway. And as she stepped between the trees, something amazing began to happen.

Rose suddenly felt as light as air. She saw the bright eyes of the bird and smelled the cool, mossy wood, but under her feet she felt nothing at all. And everything around her was becoming bigger and bigger.

It should have felt frightening, but somehow, Rose was happier than she had ever been. It was as if she was part of the woods and the flowers and the song of the bird. She found herself settling beside the bird, sitting on his branch in the sunlight.

It took Rose several minutes to understand what had happened to her. It was hard to believe that it was not just a dream. But sitting on the branch she slowly understood that she was now tiny, no bigger than the bird, and she could fly! You will have guessed much more quickly than she did—Rose had become a fairy!

"Don't worry," sang the bird. "You have always been a fairy princess. The time has come for you to know, that's all. It's not strange at all."

Part of Rose wanted to protest. It *was* strange! It was very strange indeed. She didn't usually eat breakfast and suddenly turn into a fairy! But another part of her knew that what the bird was saying was true. She felt just right. She was surprised and not surprised, all at the same time.

"You can talk to me!" said Rose, realizing that she had understood everything the bird had said.

The beautiful little bird put his head on one side. "Well," he sang, "I'm just singing, as I always do. It's simply that you can understand me now. In fact, you can hear what all living things are saying. Listen!"

It was true. All at once Rose understood that the wood was buzzing with little creatures. Not far away, a butterfly was talking to a friend. A beetle was showing his children their new home. And a daisy ... *oh!* ... a daisy was laughing!

Rose had never known that everything has its own voice. She was so keen to hear the little conversations that were going on all around her that she found herself floating gently from the branch and moving out into the glade.

"I'm flying!" laughed Rose. "And it's easy! Oh!" For a moment, thinking about flying made it difficult. Rose wobbled a little and felt as if she was falling.

"Smile and don't forget to breathe!" called the bird. "It really *is* easy!"

And Rose found that when she took a deep breath and smiled, she floated upright again. Soon she was flitting around the trees, enjoying a view of the woodland that she had never seen before.

Rose didn't know how long she spent there in the sunshine. She only knew that she felt happy. The sun was high overhead when she heard sounds from a world she had almost forgotten.

Something—no, three somethings—were crashing through the woodland. They were making a terrible noise.

"She must be here somewhere!" boomed a voice nearby. "Rose! Rose!"

It was the other princesses. Their deportment class was over, and they had come to look for their sister.

Rose, perched on a little branch high above them, looked down in horror. She didn't want to be seen, and she didn't want to go back. It was almost as if the bird could read her thoughts.

"You must go back," he said. "It is time. You can come again. You only have to follow my voice and go through the portal."

"Portal?" cried Rose. "I don't understand."

"It's just a doorway into your other life," explained the bird. "It can be a space between two trees. It can be a window, or a pool of water, or a shaft of sunlight. But whatever it is, you will know because I will be there. Come this way now. It's time to go."

Before she really understood what was happening, Rose found herself passing back between the trees. Suddenly, she was standing on the ground again, feeling huge and heavy, and being jostled by her sisters.

"Where have you been hiding?" they laughed. "You're in ever so much trouble at home."

It was true. Rose had to do an extra embroidery class and practise her minuet steps until it was almost dark.

"I don't understand," one of her sisters whispered to another. "She hates doing this. Why is she smiling?"

That night, Rose lay in her bed in her turret room and thought about everything that had happened. How long must she wait before she heard the golden bird again? Suddenly, she couldn't bear it any more. She wrapped her robe around herself and crept down the stairs, past the sleeping sentry and out into the garden. The moon was shining brightly. It was easy to find her way back into the woodland.

But among the trees it was darker. Everything looked different. Rose stumbled over stones and fallen branches. She couldn't find the trees where the golden bird had been. And there was something worse, she realized. The night-time sounds of the woodland were completely different, too. And there was no sound of singing.

Sadly, Rose walked back to the palace. She felt as if all the magic had gone from her life again, and she wasn't smiling any more.

Rose went back to her room. She lay down on her bed and closed her eyes. Shining tears slid down her cheeks. Perhaps it *had* been a dream, after all.

"Follow! Follow! Follow!"

From somewhere nearby, a silvery voice trilled through the night. Rose opened her eyes. There, sitting in a shaft of moonlight on the windowsill, was the magical bird.

Rose reached the window in a second. As her bare foot touched the moonlight on the floor, she felt once more the strange, floating feeling. She had become a fairy again!

"I'm so happy!" Rose told the bird, standing beside him. "I thought it had all been a dream. I came to look for you, and you weren't there!"

"Of course not," sang the bird. "I'm not really outside you at all. I'm inside, in your heart.

You will see me when you least expect to, but you can call me, too. If you need me, if you need to become your real self, just close your eyes and think of me. It will always work, I promise."

"I always need you!" sighed Rose. "I never want to be an ordinary princess again."

"You're not an ordinary princess," said the bird. "Surely you realize that now? You have never been an ordinary princess. You're a very special girl and you can do extraordinary things. How many girls do you know who can fly?"

Rose smiled. "No one," she whispered. "But I don't understand why this has happened to me."

"You will," promised the bird. "You will." And, as a cloud passed across the moon, and the moonlight faded, he silently disappeared.

This time, Rose didn't feel unhappy. She knew that what the bird said was true. She was smiling as she fell deeply asleep.

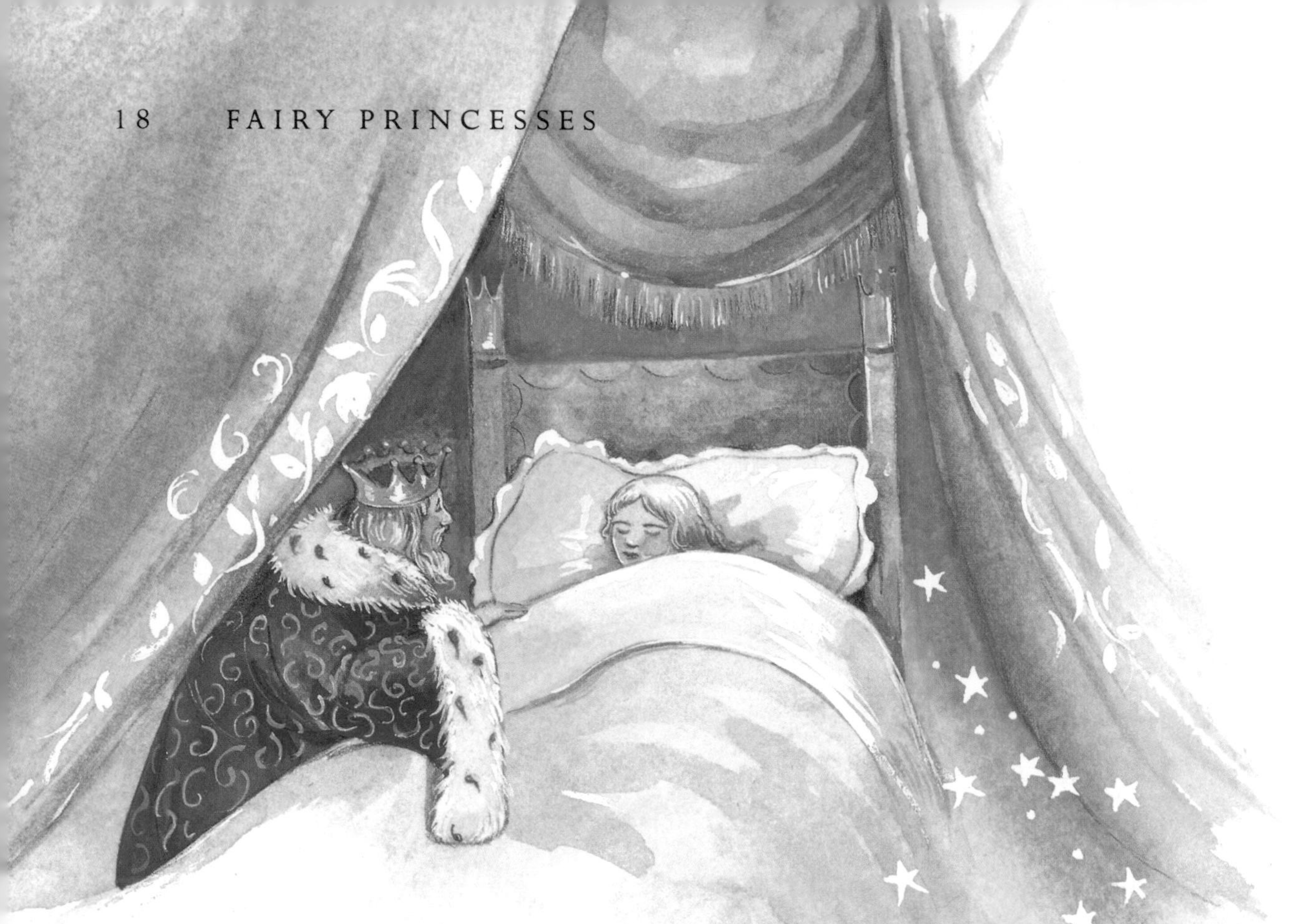

The next day, something happened that made Rose forget about being a fairy. Her mother, the Queen, was taken ill. At first, no one was concerned. As the day passed, however, the Queen grew worse. The King sent for the best doctors in the land. All night, they tended the Queen, but she grew more and more ill. Towards morning, the oldest and wisest doctor shook his head. "There is nothing more we can do," he told the King.

"Nothing?" cried the King. "Nothing at all? There must be some medicine you can give her."

The doctors exchanged glances. "There was once a little blue flower growing in this land, Sire," said one, "called the Evening Star. Juice from its petals could cure the Queen, but it has not been seen here for many years. Every single flower was picked long ago."

"If we searched...," the King began, but the doctor looked grave. "It is dark," he said. "What could anyone do? Even if the plant could be found, it would be in the most distant, hidden parts of the kingdom, and I am afraid that even by the morning, it will be too late for the Queen."

When she heard this, Rose ran from the room. "If only I could do something," she sobbed. And suddenly, she knew that she could. She thought hard about the golden bird and found herself floating into the sound of his beautiful song. She didn't need to explain. "Everyone will help," he said.

Suddenly, Rose began to hear a scurrying and a whispering all around her, as hundreds and hundreds of tiny creatures told their neighbours about the Evening Star. She felt as if she was surrounded by tiny friends.

"You are," sang the bird, as if she had spoken aloud. "Now, go back to your mother."

Well before midnight, a white dove, flying slowly on silent wings, settled on the windowsill outside the Queen's room and cooed softly. Only Rose, who had been waiting and hoping, heard the sound and ran to open the window. Quickly she went over to the wise doctor and placed something in his hands. He looked up in amazement, but Rose put her finger to her lips, and he hurried away.

In all the excitement of the Queen's recovery, no one thought to ask how the Evening Star had been found, but the bird sang in Rose's heart, and she was happy.

Princess Magnolia's Magic

When Princess Magnolia was tiny, she loved to spend the afternoons with her mother. It was very hot then, so the Queen and everyone else in the palace rested in the shade. The Queen often went to her room, where she read, or wrote letters, or slept for a while. Magnolia thought her mother was the most beautiful, wonderful woman in the world. She wanted to be just the same when she was older. So she sat quietly by the Queen and tried to do just what she did.

One afternoon, the Queen was lying on her day bed, reading, while Magnolia sat among a pile of silken cushions nearby and looked at a book, too. She couldn't read herself yet, but she loved to look at the pictures.

The Queen had some very beautiful books. Magnolia was always careful as she turned the pages. Today, Magnolia was looking at a book she had not seen before. The pictures were strange, and there were odd patterns in the margins of the pages. The little princess was enchanted by it.

Magnolia looked up as a shadow fell across her page. It was the Queen. She had an odd expression on her face.

"You've been looking at that book for a long time," she told her daughter. "Why do you like it so much?"

"I don't know," said the little girl. She grinned. "I think it's a magic book."

The Queen's eyes shone. "Magic?" she whispered. "Show me." She sat down beside Magnolia.

Gently, Magnolia turned the pages. "It's the pictures," she said. "The people in them really look at me."

"What do you mean?" Tears glittered in the Queen's eyes, but Magnolia didn't see.

"In this picture," she said, "there's a princess who smiles at me." And it was true. As the Queen looked, a girl in the picture turned her head and smiled from the page.

The Queen put her arms around her daughter.

"You are a special, special little girl," she said. "And this is our secret now. When I was young, the girl in the picture smiled at me, too. That was how I knew that I was not just an ordinary princess. I was a fairy princess. And now I can see that you are a fairy princess, too. When you are older, you will be able to do amazing things."

"We can do them together," said Magnolia. She loved her mother so much, she wasn't a bit surprised to find that she could do magic.

But the Queen sighed. "No," she said. "I am not a fairy princess any more. I am a queen now. I don't have magic powers any longer."

"*I* think you're magic!" said Magnolia, hugging her mother.

Time passed, and Magnolia grew prettier every day. But she still couldn't do magic, and she began to think that she wasn't a fairy princess after all. Her mother found her one day staring at her schoolbooks. Magnolia slammed a book down in disgust. "I'm not magic at all," she pouted. "I've been trying to say a spell to do my sums for me. It didn't work!"

"I'm not surprised," said the Queen. "Didn't you know that you can only do magic if it helps someone else? You can never do magic to help yourself."

"But when will I learn?"

"You won't start doing magic when *you* want to," her mother replied. "The magic has to come to you. It happens in a special way, but I can't help. It will happen when it happens."

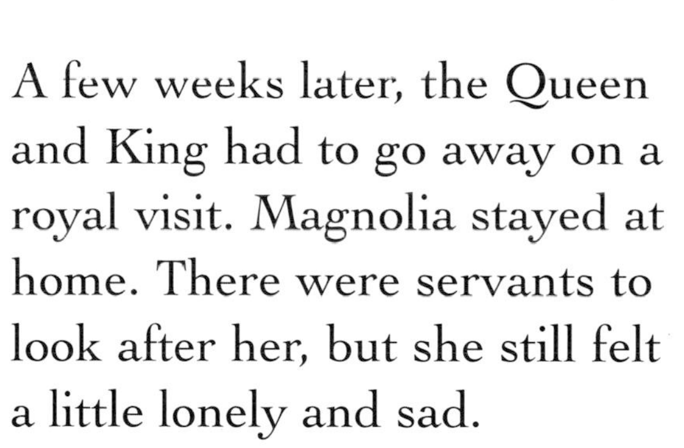

A few weeks later, the Queen and King had to go away on a royal visit. Magnolia stayed at home. There were servants to look after her, but she still felt a little lonely and sad.

One evening, as Magnolia sat alone in her room, she heard a beautiful sound. It was a bird, singing his heart out. Magnolia ran to the window, but there was no sign of a bird in the golden light of evening. Besides, the sound seemed to be coming from inside the room. Magnolia turned. Something strange was happening … at last! On the walls of the room were painted flowers and birds and twirling vines. One golden bird was singing!

Magnolia hardly had time to feel excited. She walked towards the bird. The song began to swirl around her. It was as if the music was sweeping her up. She couldn't feel the floor beneath her feet. She was flying! "It's magic!" cried Magnolia, joyfully.

"Now you are a fairy princess," sang the bird, "the whole world will be magic for you."

Magnolia looked around. She was whirling across the room, and all around her wonderful things were happening. Flowers were blooming on the walls. Stars were shimmering all around. Magnolia swept her hand through the air, and rose petals fell from her fingertips.

"This is your magic," sang the bird. "You can make things beautiful wherever you go. Wherever you find me, I will lead you into your very own magical world."

In the morning, Princess Magnolia woke on a pile of satin cushions and wondered if it had all been a dream. But when she looked around, the walls were still covered with beautiful flowers, and there were rose petals on the floor.

Magnolia stood up. She felt heavy and awkward. She couldn't fly, and when she waved her hand, nothing magical happened at all. Then she remembered that she must find the bird to help her. But strangely, all the birds on the walls had their heads turned.

Magnolia listened as hard as she could, but there was no singing to be heard. She felt very sorry for herself.

Magnolia spent the next few weeks in a kind of daze. She was so unsure about what had happened that she didn't even tell her mother about it. She could think of nothing but her own disappointment.

The Queen could tell that something was wrong, but the flowers had faded from the walls. She did not know what had happened to her daughter.

"Next time we have to go away," she told her husband, "we must take Magnolia, too. It isn't good for a young girl to be left alone."

So it happened that a month or so later, the royal party set off to visit the farthest region of the kingdom. Magnolia was quiet and sad, as she had been since the summer. All went well, until one night, when rain lashed down and wild winds blew, the royal party was forced to shelter in a town at the foot of the mountains.

The next morning, the day dawned grey but fine. Magnolia stepped out into the watery light and was shocked by what she saw. The town was pitiful. Buildings were broken and battered. A grey dust filled the streets, the gardens and even the houses. Worse than that, the people themselves looked grey and defeated. They seemed to have lost all hope and were simply dragging themselves from day to day.

When Magnolia's parents appeared, a local man explained that a volcano had erupted a year before, covering everything in its deadly ash. Now nothing would grow, and the town itself was dying.

Magnolia felt as though her heart would break. Suddenly, she had no thought for herself at all. Behind her, she could hear her parents hurrying away to discuss with their officials what could be done to help these people, but they were talking of weeks and months and years.

Then Magnolia noticed a little bird, scratching in the dust. And as she watched, it turned towards her. Surely, beneath the grey, it was a golden bird? Magnolia reached out her hand, very gently and carefully. The bird bent its head for a moment, and then it sang!

Magnolia felt herself whirling in the swirl of sound. She stretched out her arms, and suddenly, wonderful things began to happen. From the dust, flowers began to bloom. Grey faces lifted and smiled. And all the birds in the town began to sing.

Magnolia smiled, too. At last she understood what being a fairy princess was all about.

Princess Daisy's Darkness

There was once a princess who was afraid of the dark. She didn't know why she was afraid, but at night she insisted that the lamp beside her bed should be kept burning. It didn't help that Princess Daisy lived in a northern country, where summer days were light until very late, but winter days were almost as dark as night. Daisy dreaded the winters and longed for the summer light. Then, when summer came, she could not enjoy it because she knew that winter would come again.

It was during the summer that Princess Daisy first discovered she was a fairy princess. She was walking through the pinewoods with her dog on a bright, sunny day. The trees were shady, but here and there, golden pools of sunlight shimmered on the path. Daisy and Tor, the dog, played a game, chasing each other from one patch of sunlight to the next. At last, laughing but out of breath, Daisy threw herself down to rest under a tree. Tor flopped down beside her.

At first, all they could hear was their own breathing. Then, quite suddenly, a bird began to sing nearby. It was the most beautiful sound that Daisy had ever heard.

Daisy looked around. She spotted the singer sitting on a branch in a shaft of sunlight. He seemed to glow gold in the light. Daisy had never seen such a bird before.

Then Princess Daisy noticed something very strange. Tor was trotting away through the trees. Usually, he never left her side. Daisy always felt safe with Tor. Now he was leaving, yet she didn't feel frightened at all. In fact, the song of the bird seemed to be filling her with a golden happiness. Daisy was not at all surprised when she rose lightly into the air and above the trees, out into the sunlight above.

Daisy could see the forest stretching away. She could see the mountains in the distance. Above the trees, the turrets of her castle home sparkled and shone. "The bird will look after me," Daisy thought.

"No-o," the bird's song floated up. "You'll look after yourself!"

It was true! Daisy found that she only had to concentrate a little bit to fly wherever she wanted. High in the bright air, she didn't ever want to go back amongst the trees.

Suddenly, from far below, Daisy heard a dreadful howling sound. It was Tor! Daisy could tell at once that he was frightened and in pain, and soon she knew why. It was as though the handsome dog was speaking to her.

"He's caught in a trap!" gasped Daisy, and she flew down towards the sound. It was only when she flew past the first branches of the trees that Daisy realized something she had not noticed before. She was tiny! Somehow, when the bird sang, she had become much smaller.

But Daisy didn't have time to think about her size. Tor's howls were becoming fainter. At last, the princess fluttered down beside her dog. His paw was caught in a vicious, metal trap. His head was lying on the mossy ground, and his eyes were closed.

Daisy went at once to open the trap, but it would have been impossible even at her normal size. Now there was nothing she could do. Tears ran down Daisy's face. Tor was going to die, and she could not help.

"You can do it! Magic is all you need!" sang the bird. Daisy lifted her head. Whatever could it mean? She didn't know how to do magic. She felt hopeless.

The bird was singing again. "You didn't know how to fly, either. How did you do that?"

Daisy thought quickly. "I don't know," she whispered. "And I don't know how to do this either, but I will try."

She closed her eyes and imagined Tor running free across a hillside. *Snap!* The iron hinges fell apart, but Tor lay still. Daisy knew that she could not lift him, but somehow she had to get help. Again, she closed her eyes.

She imagined men running through the forest, looking for her and the dog. Almost as soon as the picture had flashed through her head, she heard a thundering of feet and shouts as her father's woodmen ran into the clearing.

In a flash, Daisy fluttered into the trees. She didn't know how she could explain that she had changed. She needn't have worried. As the men bent over the dog, Daisy felt a heaviness and found herself sinking to the ground. She was her real size again.

It took a long time for Tor to recover from his wounds. Daisy looked after him every day. At night, he slept by her bed. She was so busy thinking about Tor that she hardly noticed summer passing. Of course, from time to time she wondered about the extraordinary things that had happened to her. She began to think it had all been a dream.

Then, one evening, there was a coolness in the air, and Daisy noticed that it was getting dark. She felt a great sadness well up inside her. That night she whispered to Tor, "You love the summer as much as I do. I wish the winter would not come for us."

Suddenly, outside the window, she heard a bird singing. Then another, and another. She threw open her heavy curtains. It was no longer dark outside! The summer had returned!

Princess Daisy slept well that night, with her windows open to the garden and the soft light of a summer night falling on her pillow. In the morning, she put on a cotton dress and ran happily down to breakfast.

She realized at once that no one else felt the same. Her parents frowned and looked worried.

"It's not right," said her mother. "Something dreadful is going to happen. I know it!"

"I will summon my wisest advisers," replied the King. "They will know why this has happened."

The servants scuttled about their business, not daring to look up. They were frightened. They didn't understand why winter had suddenly turned into summer.

There were other problems, too. In the forests, animals were found, ill and distressed, beside the paths. Great bears and tiny mice, who usually spent the winter asleep in caves and among tree roots, had been woken by the light. They did not know what to do.

In the gardens, trees turned yellow and branches drooped.

"Poor things, they need their winter's rest," said the Queen. "I'm afraid we shall lose many of them."

Princess Daisy felt guilty and sad. She knew in her heart that it was her magic that had changed winter to summer. Although she loved the sunshine so much, she knew what she must do.

Princess Daisy tried wishing, but nothing happened. Why had she been able to wish for winter to end but now could not make it return? There was only one thing to do. She must find the bird and ask his advice.

Daisy wandered into the woods and listened for the song that had filled her with happiness all those months before. She heard nothing. Even the ordinary birdsong sounded somehow wrong. Daisy ran back to the castle and called for Tor.

"You can find the bird, Tor," she whispered, stroking his rough coat. The faithful dog put his head on one side and set off towards the forest. He led Daisy further than she had ever been before.

It was gloomy among the trees. The princess felt uneasy. Then, suddenly, she heard the song she had longed for.

The golden bird was singing as if its heart would break. Daisy burst into tears. "I'm sorry," she whispered.

"I'm sorry, too," sang the bird. "Do not be afraid of the darkness, dear child. We need these quiet times, just as we need to sleep and rest."

"I know that now," said Daisy quietly. "I will never use magic again if you can put this right."

"You were born to use magic," the bird seemed to say. "You just need to learn how to use it properly. I can teach you. Now, you can help me to bring back the winter, but we will do it slowly, so that the plants and animals are not afraid."

So it was that the days grew colder, and the nights grew darker, and everything was back as it should be. Daisy had learned to love the darkness and to use her magic wisely, and the kingdom was happy once more.

The Princesses' Presents

All families are magical in their own way, but some families are more magical than others. King Constant had seven daughters, and *all* of them were fairy princesses. This sometimes made life very difficult for the King, who had no idea at all how to do magic himself.

The eldest princess was called Aurelia. She was seventeen at the time of this story. Her sisters were Bella (fifteen), Claudia (thirteen), Delia (eleven), Eugenia (nine), Fiona (seven), and Giggles (five). Giggles' real name was Georgina, but no one ever called her that.

The princesses had a problem. It wasn't a horrible problem, but it was a problem all the same. King Constant had a Very Big Birthday in a month's time. The princesses wanted to give him a Really Special Present, but they couldn't decide what it should be.

"I think he'd like a dolls' house," said Giggles. "A really big one, looking like our palace, with little dolls inside looking like us!"

The older girls frowned. "That's not what *he* would like," they said. "That's what *you* would like!" Giggles had to admit this was true, though she still thought it was a good present for anyone!

"I think he'd like a horse," suggested Bella. "A white stallion from the hills. They would look wonderful at parades."

"Father likes his old horse," said Aurelia. "A stallion from the hills might be, well, livelier than he could manage at his age."

The girls agreed. They thought the King was about to be Very Old Indeed.

"I know what he would really like," said Fiona quietly. "He'd like a holiday. A real holiday without any parades, or people shaking his hand, or trumpets, or banquets. He'd like to wear old clothes and not have to think about being the King."

All the princesses turned to look at Fiona. This really was a very good idea. Their father often looked tired, and official holidays always involved lots of parades, and people shaking his hand, and trumpets, and banquets. A proper holiday was just what he needed for his Very Big Birthday.

"Well, there's only one thing to decide," said Aurelia. "Where should we send him?"

"Tahiti!" cried Bella. "He'd love the sunshine."

"Switzerland!" shouted Claudia. "He's always wanted to learn to ski."

"Brazil!" yelled Delia. "He could paddle down the Amazon and have adventures."

"Australia!" Eugenia was sure she had the answer. "He could go surfing. No one would recognize him in shorts!"

"China!" Fiona had seen pictures of the Great Wall. She knew her father would love to say he had walked along it.

Giggles hadn't studied as much geography as her sisters. "The Moon!" she screeched, to drown out the others. "In a rocket!"

Aurelia, as the eldest, felt it was her job to make a decision. It was difficult. "I think he'd love all those places," she said slowly. "And Egypt, which was my idea. Do you think we should ask him where he would really like to go?"

"NO!" chorused the other girls. "It has to be a surprise. It's not a Really Special Present if he knows about it."

Aurelia admitted that this was true. "Maybe we could find out without exactly asking," she said. "We could be clever about it. That means you keep quiet, Giggles!"

The King was busy all that day, and it was late when he came home. The princesses decided that breakfast the next morning might be the best time to try to find out where he would really like to go.

One by one, the princesses went to bed. The King, tired from saluting and shaking hands, retired to his royal bedchamber as well. Quietness reigned in the palace, and in the empty corridors, only a few lanterns glimmered.

But no one was having a peaceful night! In their rooms, the princesses tossed and turned. Princess Aurelia wished she had tried harder to persuade her sisters that Egypt was the best place. She could so vividly imagine the King strolling under palm trees beside the River Nile, or swaying along on a camel with the Pyramids in the distance.

Bella and Claudia shared a room. They were whispering together in the darkness. "I think you might be right about Switzerland," hissed Bella. "I've always wanted to learn to ski, too. Perhaps we could go with him. Anyway, can't you imagine the King whizzing down a mountain? He'd love it!"

"I know," whispered Claudia sharply. "That's why I suggested it!"

Both girls lay awake, gazing into the darkness, imagining the fun their father (and his daughters) would have in the Alps.

Delia and Eugenia shared, too, but they could not agree. "There are huge snakes in the Amazon," Delia enthused.

"Well, he wouldn't like *that*!" growled Eugenia. "They're dangerous!"

"There are sharks and poisonous spiders in Australia," Delia reminded her. "What makes you think he'd want to see *them*?"

Eugenia suddenly had a vision of her father being pursued by a great white shark. She brushed the thought away. "A shark wouldn't dare to try to eat a king," she said, hoping this was true.

In their room, Fiona and Giggles were not at all worried by little details like geography and the frontiers of science. "He could go to China first," said Fiona, "then fly from there to the Moon. We could look out at night and wave to him. He could be King of the Moon!"

"And we could be Moon Princesses," said Giggles. "That would be lovely. I can just imagine my shiny moony dress."

Awake in their beds, all the princesses were imagining. Poor King Constant! You see, when fairy princesses think hard enough about something, especially something that is good for someone else, it very often happens. While the princesses thought and dreamed, the King was hurtling around the world, in the snow one minute and the ocean the next. He'd just got used to strolling beside the Nile when he was whisked off to the Moon! No sooner had he begun to feel comfortable there than he found himself nose to fang with a deadly snake! It was dreadful! And all in his best royal pyjamas!

Knowing nothing of this, the princesses arrived at breakfast the next morning, determined to find out where their father would most like to be taken on holiday.

"Dearest Papa," Aurelia began, "you are looking tired. Wouldn't you like a little holiday?"

Then she rubbed her eyes and looked again. Her father really *was* looking tired. In fact, it was as if he hadn't slept in weeks!

"Are you quite well, Papa?" she asked.

"No, I'm not!" cried the King. "I feel as though I've been dragged around the world all night long. I never want to see a foreign country again! Or the Moon!"

The princesses exchanged guilty glances. They guessed what had happened. They were disappointed, too. Giggles, who had not yet learnt to be tactful, blurted out what they had all been thinking. "But now we can't send you on holiday for your birthday!"

The King looked around at seven sad faces. Although he didn't really understand about magic or what had happened, he hated to see his daughters so unhappy.

"Well, there is one thing I would really love for my birthday," he said, "and that is to have my portrait painted with the most beautiful princesses in the world. Yes, I mean *you*!"

Well, Giggles found it hard to keep still, and Bella would keep talking, but no one met a poisonous snake or a shark, and everyone was happy with the result.

Princess Nerina's Problem

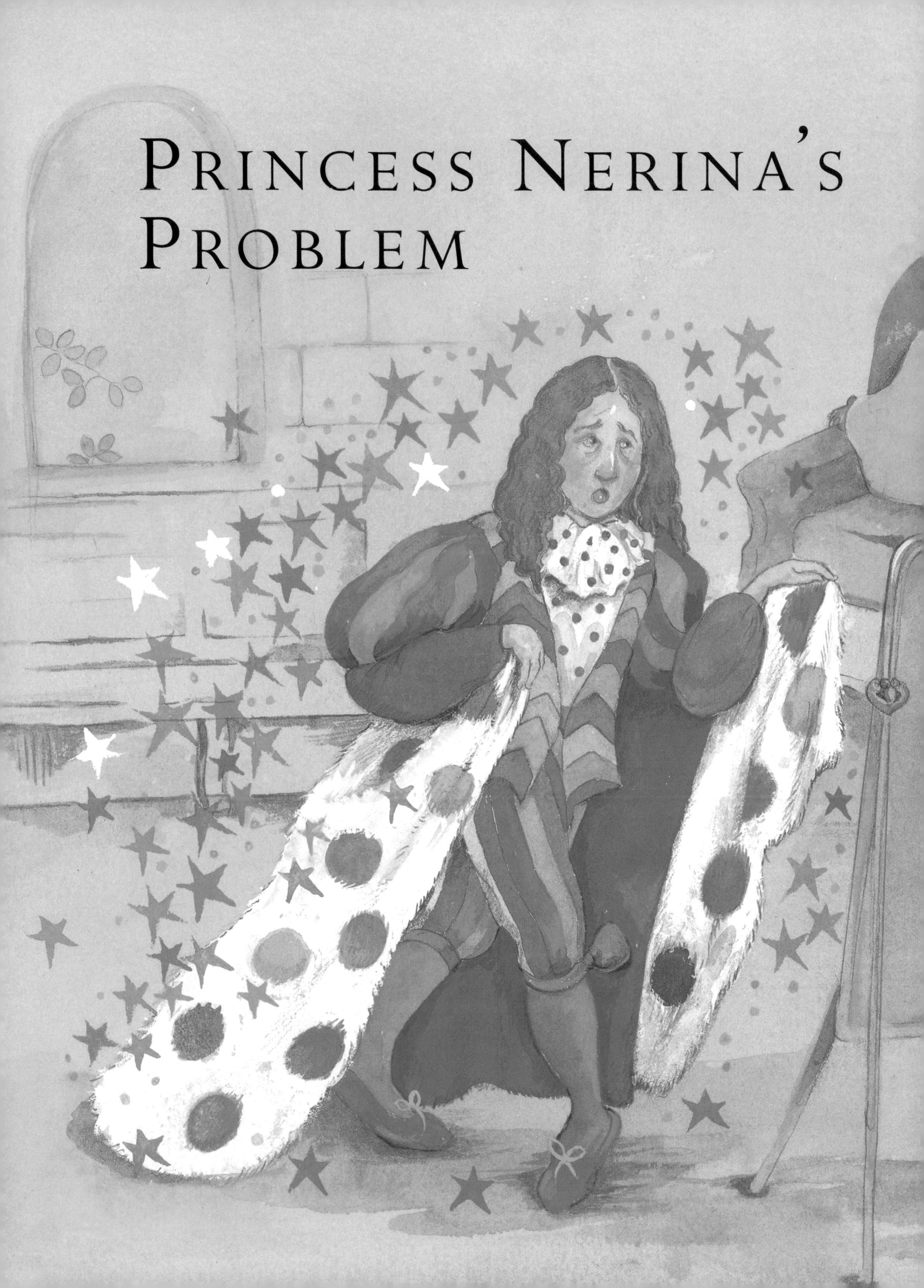

Princess Nerina discovered that she was a fairy princess when she was very small. She loved it! Although she knew that she should use her magical powers to help people, she soon realized that she could have a lot of fun as well. One morning, as she watched her father put on his kingly robes, she began to wonder what they would look like if they were more interesting than the usual royal red. No sooner had the idea drifted into her head than the robes became quite extraordinary!

Nerina concentrated hard and put things right straight away. The King decided he had been imagining things and must get more sleep.

After that, Nerina had a lot of fun decorating her bedroom. It was brilliant! Not only was it the most gorgeous room in the house, but when she heard her mother coming down the corridor, she could quickly magic it back to pink and purple.

As she grew older, Nerina grew bolder! One day, walking in the gardens, she suddenly decided to change all the domes on the palace. Usually a simple pale green shade, they looked wonderful in purple, gold, orange and pink. A passing pigeon fluttered down in shock. The princess sighed happily, until she heard her mother's voice. "Nerina! Change those domes back at once! What would your father think?"

Nerina jumped. She thought she had been alone. The Queen was marching across the lawn. She certainly did not look happy.

"Now look here, Nerina," she said, "I know you love to do magic. I did, too, at your age. But you must be more discreet. Not everyone is happy about this kind of thing. Your father would prefer to believe that magic doesn't exist. It worries him. Now please be more careful in future."

Nerina promised. She sometimes changed the flowers in the ballroom from white to pink (when no one was there, of course). She once sat at a very, very boring banquet and amused herself by changing her underwear from green to orange to purple to red all through dinner without anyone knowing at all!

Princesses are not often alone. They are usually surrounded by courtiers and servants, or waving to crowds of people. But everyone needs to be alone sometimes, so Nerina loved to ride out on her horse Palmira. At first her father insisted that soldiers and servants went with her, but after a while his daughter persuaded him to let her ride across the wide, open grasslands by herself.

It was on these rides that Princess Nerina got into the bad habit of having fun with her magic when she thought no one could see. Palmira was a beautiful grey horse, but when she was out of sight of the palace, Nerina changed her to a gleaming jet black. Palmira seemed to like it. She tossed her head and galloped faster.

This gave Nerina an idea. She changed her own long, blonde hair to jet black, too. The girl and her horse looked very striking, riding like the wind across the bending grasses, hair and mane and tail streaming out behind them.

That was the sight that caught the eye of Prince Averne, riding home himself from a visit to his grandmother. The moment that he saw the amazing girl on her wonderful horse, he decided that he must marry her. She was unlike anyone he had ever seen.

Nerina, speeding by, didn't even notice the young man, but Averne had seen the coronet on her saddlecloth. That night he presented himself at the royal palace.

The King greeted him, as one royal person should greet another, and asked how he could help his visitor. Prince Averne came straight to the point. "I would like to marry your daughter," he said.

"I confess that I saw her today as she rode across the plain, and I do not think that I can live without her. My family is a good one, as you know, and I will inherit my parents' kingdom one day. You can ask anyone about me. I feel sure that I would be a good husband for her, and you can be sure that I would always love and care for her."

The King was startled. It was true that Nerina was now old enough to be married, but it hadn't occurred to him that the event would happen so soon. The young man seemed ideal, but there were other things to consider. One thing in particular.

The King cleared his throat. "For what it is worth," he said, "I should be delighted to welcome you as a son-in-law, but this is not a decision for me to make. The princess must say herself whom she will marry. However, I see no harm in introducing you."

The King hurried off to tell his wife what had happened. Together, they rushed to Nerina's room. On the way, they agreed that too many details might put her off. "Just a casual meeting," said the King. "Who knows, she might be as smitten by him as he obviously is by her."

When the Queen had finished fussing over Nerina's hair, the royal family arrived back in the receiving room. The prince looked up eagerly.

"May I present my daughter, the Princess Nerina," the King announced. Nerina, seeing a most handsome young man before her, made her very best curtsey. She certainly did like what she saw.

But the prince took a step backwards. "I'm sorry," he said, "but there has been some misunderstanding. Oh dear, this is embarrassing. It is your other daughter I mean. The one with raven hair who rides a magnificent black horse."

The King and Queen looked at each other in puzzlement. Nerina gulped and tried to look innocent, while furiously thinking about what to do. While the King and Queen explained that she was their only daughter, and the prince apologized for troubling them as politely as he could, Princess Nerina was able to look at him more carefully and listen to him talking. He was desperately handsome, funny and clever, she decided. What could she do?

Bowing low, the prince backed out of the room. "I'll show him out," gasped Nerina, and before her parents could speak, she had seized the prince's arm and dragged him into the corridor.

I simply cannot let him go, thought Nerina. I will simply have to tell him the truth. He is young. Surely he can't be bothered about magic? As quickly as she could, Nerina explained that it had been she with raven hair and a magnificent black horse.

Prince Averne looked thunderstruck. Was the girl mad? "Don't they have magic in your country?" cried Nerina. The prince shook his head, backing away again.

Princess Nerina decided that desperate circumstances needed desperate deeds. She pulled the prince under a chandelier and in an instant changed herself into the girl he had seen that morning. The poor prince almost fainted, the shock was so great.

"Or you might prefer this!" cried Nerina desperately. In an instant she had orange hair, blue hair and purple hair. In her panic, she didn't concentrate and gave herself a green face as well. It wasn't an attractive look. The prince's face became more and more concerned. With a strangled cry, he turned and ran.

Poor Nerina fled to her bedroom and refused to come out for three days. The more she thought about Prince Averne, the surer she became that she wanted to spend her life with him. But it was dreadful that he was disgusted by her magical powers.

In desperation, Nerina went to her mother. "I don't want to be a fairy princess any more," she said. "There must be something I can do to give up my powers."

The Queen smiled. "I imagine that this has something to do with a certain prince," she said. "You know, there is nothing to worry about. When you are married, your magic will disappear quite naturally, just as mine did when I married your father. It has always been that way. Your only problem, my girl, is finding a way to let Prince Averne know that."

In the end, there was no problem. Prince Averne, too, had shut himself in his room for days. When his mother asked what was wrong, the story came tumbling out.

"I like the sound of your Princess Nerina," said the Queen. Then she told him just what Nerina's mother had told her. "I was a fairy princess myself once," she said. "So I know."

So it was that Prince Averne once more rode out towards the palace of the girl he loved. At this meeting, Nerina controlled herself. As a matter of fact, she was so busy staring into her prince's blue eyes that she didn't even think about doing magic. Two days later, both kingdoms were rejoicing at the news of the royal engagement, and fairy princesses from far and wide looked forward to the wedding.

Many Kinds of Magic

Most invitations to the wedding of Princess Nerina and Prince Averne were sent by messenger or mail. They were written in gold on thick, cream card, with the crests of both families at the top. Royal families far and near eagerly waited for their arrival. Some special invitations, however, were not sent but sung. A certain golden bird made sure that fairy princesses everywhere knew of the wedding long before anyone else.

So it was that two days before the wedding, all the rooms of Princess Nerina's palace and several of the grander houses nearby were filled with royal guests and the many servants they felt they needed to bring.

All seemed set for a wonderful wedding day until the King's Weather Watcher, a very old man with a long, white beard, asked to see His Majesty.

"Well, really," cried the King, who was having final adjustments made to his royal robes, "I'm much too busy to see him now. Tell him to come back on Thursday."

But the old man sent back a message at once to say that Thursday would be too late. Much, much too late.

"Very well," sighed the King. "Send him in. But he only has two minutes. I need to consult with the royal cooks again."

The Weather Watcher shuffled into the room. "Sire," he said, "I fear that I have bad news."

It seemed that a blizzard of huge proportions was heading towards the palace from the mountains far away across the plains.

The King went pale. Then he strode quickly around the room, looking out of each of the many windows of the tower room. In every direction, the sky was blue and sunny.

The King didn't wish to be unkind. "My dear old fellow, you have worked hard for me for more years than I can remember. Perhaps it is time you retired," he said. "After the wedding we can have a little party for you. How about it?"

The old man tried to protest, but the King had too much on his mind to worry about something as unlikely as a blizzard.

He sent the Weather Watcher away and thought no more about snow … until he woke up the next morning.

For that night, when everyone was asleep—even the boy who kept the lanterns alight in the palace courtyards—more visitors came to the palace. They were little white, whirling visitors, swirling thick and fast from the inky sky. In an hour, the gardens and roofs were covered with a crisp, white layer that sparkled in the moonlight. In two hours, doorways were blocked and paths filled knee-deep with snow. By the time the lantern-boy awoke, and the cockerels were stirring on the royal farm, the whole kingdom was unrecognizable.

As far as the eye could see, the world was white. It looked beautiful, but it was, for a king planning a wedding, disastrous. On the day that should have been one of the happiest of his life, the King sat with his head in his hands, too anxious even to pace up and down.

Every road in the kingdom was blocked. Nothing and no one could reach the palace. And on the day of the royal wedding, there was a very great deal that needed to reach the palace.

The Queen, trying to be practical, made a list of everything that was lacking for the ceremony. It didn't make her or her husband feel any better.

most of the food
most of the wine
flowers for the cathedral
trimmings for Nerina's dress
musicians
white horses for carriages
open roads for carriages
and last but not least...
Prince Averne!

"Where is he exactly?" groaned the King, referring to his future son-in-law.

"Only two miles away, but it might as well be two hundred," replied the Queen. "We could manage, perhaps, without the other things, but you cannot have a wedding without a groom!"

Princess Nerina was even more upset. She sat in her room in despair, using her magic to turn everything she owned black or purple or a hideous shade of green to suit her mood. In a much smaller room opposite, another princess watched with interest as the curtains she could see from her window changed colour. It was Princess Rose, who had travelled to the palace with her sisters and parents a few days earlier. She realized at once that the snow would cause big problems for the expected wedding.

I wish I could help, she thought, but my magic is not great enough to solve all the trouble this snow has brought. Just then, she heard a familiar sound. A golden voice was singing from just outside the window. At once, Rose understood what the bird was telling her.

"There are more of us!" she gasped. "Of course! Why didn't I realize that? If Nerina is a fairy princess and I am one, there must be others, too. And some of them are here!"

At the very same moment, in another part of the castle, the seven fairy daughters of King Constant had realized the same thing. As you will remember, when those girls think about something, it tends to happen. In an instant, their room was full of princesses—very special ones! All of them had been brought there by the power of the girls' magical thoughts.

"What's happening?" Nerina was not pleased. She looked in astonishment at the other princesses. Most of them she had never met before.

Princess Rose was there, of course. She quickly realized what had happened and looked around with interest at the other girls. The seven princess sisters smiled as they were joined by Princesses Magnolia and Daisy, too. As the eldest visitor, Princess Aurelia decided it was up to her to take charge. She clapped her hands.

"Your Royal Highnesses," she began. "I think I understand what is happening here. Like you, my sisters and I are fairy princesses. I think we can all guess that we are here to help Princess Nerina on her special day. Let's introduce ourselves to each other for a few moments and then settle down to work out what we can do."

There was a buzz of excitement in the room. Eleven fairy princesses hurried around the room, greeting each other. Little Princess Georgina (usually known as Giggles) felt that there were more important things to be done. She shut her eyes hard and imagined drinks and cookies, which magically appeared at a long table at one end of the room.

"Well done, Giggles," whispered Aurelia, as the princesses all began to gather around the table.

As the princesses took their places, everyone turned to Aurelia once more, but she shook her head. "This is Princess Nerina's palace," she said, "and it is her special day. She should be in charge."

It was Nerina's turn to smile. "Not at all," she said. "I am so nervous and worried that I can't think straight." The fact that the plate of cookies in front of her immediately turned a ghastly shade of green proved this!

Princess Aurelia nodded gravely. "Then I will speak," she said, "but I would like everyone else to add their own ideas."

Aurelia took a sip of her drink. "Now," she said, "the first thing we need to do is to find out exactly what the biggest problems are."

"I can help you there," sighed Nerina. "My mother has made a list. Look!" And she showed the other princesses what her mother had written.

"We'll start at the beginning," said Aurelia. "It seems that a lot of food is stuck in villages nearby but has not yet reached the palace. What can we do about that?"

For the first time, Princess Nerina looked a little less anxious. "Well, the smallest princess here has already shown how good she is at magicking a feast," she said. "Perhaps she could help?"

Giggles looked ready to burst with pride, but she was worried that preparing a huge wedding banquet might not be quite as easy as conjuring up some drinks and cookies. Her sisters Bella, Claudia, Delia and Eugenia came to stand beside her. "We will help Giggles," they said. "If the royal chef could give us the menu for this evening, we will see what we can do."

"That is easily arranged," Nerina promised.

"Now," Aurelia glanced at the list, "we seem to have no wine, either. Giggles is much too young to have anything to do with that."

Princess Nerina was looking happier every moment. "I can help with that, too," she said. "There is plenty of wine in the palace cellars, but it is of the very best kind. My father was not planning to serve it to the hundreds of guests here today. But if I tell him he must do it for the wedding of his only daughter, then I am sure he will. Cross that off your list, too, Aurelia!"

Aurelia smiled. "We are doing well," she commented, "but the next two items are more difficult. We need flowers for the cathedral, which is luckily nearby, and trimmings for Nerina's dress. They were to have been flowers, too."

"My dress could be plain," sighed Nerina. "It is not the most important thing in the world."

"But it is!" Little Princess Magnolia spoke for the first time. "You must look beautiful on your wedding day. I can see that there are no flowers to be found around the palace, now that the snow has come, but I think I can help. I will dance for you."

"My dear, you are very kind, but how will that help?" asked Nerina.

Magnolia simply said, "Watch!"

She got up from her seat and gracefully twirled across the room. As she went, the carpet bloomed with roses, and rose petals began to fall like snowflakes from the ceiling.

The other princesses clapped their hands delightedly. "This is going to be the most beautiful wedding there has ever been!" cried Nerina, with tears in her eyes.

Aurelia's eyes were back on the list. "The musicians are not yet here," she said gravely. "A wedding without music would be a sad event."

The princesses sat in silence. Suddenly a pure, golden song came from the windowsill. It was the magical bird, and at the sound of his voice, Princess Rose looked up and laughed.

"Of course!" she exclaimed. "I am able to understand all the tiny creatures of the world, and to speak to them, too. I will summon all the birds in the kingdom. The snow will not stop them from flying to us. You will have the loveliest music on earth, Nerina."

Aurelia was feeling more confident as she read the next two items on the list. "The white horses, which come, I believe from the plains far away," she said, "are not yet here. And even if they *were* here, the roads are impassable. Although the cathedral is nearby, a princess cannot walk to her wedding. How are the royal carriages to get through the streets?"

"I can help with that," said Princess Daisy. "My magic enables me to change the seasons. I learned my lesson once when I tried to stop the winter from coming. Everything went wrong, and no one was truly happy. I would not like to try to magic away all the snow, but I think I could clear it away from the courtyards and the road to the cathedral. In fact, I have an idea of what we might do with all the snow that would need to be moved."

"That still leaves us with the problem of the white horses," said Aurelia.

"There are plenty of carriage horses in the royal stables," Nerina replied, "and I can make them white in an instant. That is not at all difficult. Now, Aurelia, aren't you forgetting the most important problem of all?"

"Not at all!" Aurelia was grinning now. "My sisters and I can transport many people a short distance, which is how you all come to be here now, but we can also transport one person a long distance. Just ask my father! I myself will make sure that Prince Averne is here in time. Now, my dears, there is so much to do. Let us be busy. In five hours' time, Princess Nerina is to be married!"

The King was amazed to see his daughter, who an hour before had looked unhappier than he had ever seen her, smiling as she ran along the corridor towards her room.

"Why aren't you getting ready, Father?" she called. "Don't you know I'm getting married today? It's going to be the most wonderful wedding ever!"

It was true. No one who was there could ever forget the wedding of Prince Averne and Princess Nerina. In the banqueting hall, an amazing feast awaited the guests. The road to the cathedral still had a light covering of snow, but the carriages passed over it with ease. And along the route, beautiful columns and arches had been built with the snow that had been cleared away.

Nerina's carriage was pulled by perfect white horses, and her dress, when she stood on the steps of the cathedral to wave to the people, was wonderfully decorated with flowers of white and the palest pink. Drops of dew sparkled like diamonds among the petals.

In fact, there were flowers everywhere. Magnolia had danced as she had never danced before. The cathedral was full of beautiful blooms, while festoons of blossoms were draped over buildings and carriages.

Among the flowers, tiny songbirds filled the air with the most beautiful music.

Everyone was amazed by the magnificence of the event, but Prince Averne was the most surprised of all. One moment he was sitting sadly by his window, watching the hands of the stable clock tick slowly towards the hour when he should be by his bride's side. The next moment, he was standing in the cathedral, watching the most beautiful girl in the world float down the aisle towards him.

Of course, the fairy princesses were bridesmaids, and as they followed Princess Nerina and her husband out into the sunshine, their hearts sang with the birds fluttering overhead. The crowd outside burst into applause.

It was then that Giggles, looking down at the carriage awaiting the newly married couple, gasped, "Oh no! Nerina has forgotten to make the horses white again!"

Princess Aurelia bent down. "She hasn't forgotten, sweetheart," she said. "It's just that now that she is married, she cannot be a fairy princess like us any more, and she cannot do magic."

"Oh, that is so sad!" cried Giggles. "Poor Nerina!"

But Nerina, who was gazing up at her new husband with sparkling eyes, heard the little girl's cry. Still smiling up at her prince, she said softly, "No, it's not sad. This is another kind of magic."